Magical Rescue Vets

Blaze the Phoenix

Books in the Magical Rescue Vets series

Oona the Unicorn
Jade the Gem Dragon
Blaze the Phoenix
Holly the Flying Horse

This edition published in 2022 by Arcturus Publishing Limited
26/27 Bickels Yard, 151–153 Bermondsey Street,
London SE1 3HA

Author: Melody Lockhart
Illustrator: Morgan Huff
Story editor: Claudia Martin
Project editors: Joe Harris and Xanna Eve Chown
Designer: Jeni Child

CH007647NT
Supplier 10, Date 0422, PI 00000577

Printed in the UK

Contents

Starfall Forest Map

Chapter 1
A Baby Grumpling

"Rosie! Are you listening?"

Rosie jumped as she suddenly remembered where she was. "Ooh, I'm sorry, Miss Lavender," she gasped.

It was Friday. She was in her new school in Springhaven. Outside, the sun was shining on the schoolyard, but Rosie had been daydreaming about the enchanted place that lay beyond it. Starfall Forest was home to the most extraordinary magical creatures —and it was where she and her best friend Kat had spent most of the summer, having amazing adventures.

Miss Lavender bent over Rosie's book and looked at the tidy row of sums. "This is nice work," she said. "You must have had a good teacher at your old school."

"I did," said Rosie, smiling. Her family had only moved to Springhaven a short while ago, but her time in Opal City already felt like a lifetime away.

As Miss Lavender walked over to another student, Rosie's eyes were drawn back to the window and the white clouds that were sailing across the blue sky.

"That one looks like a flutterpuff," thought Rosie, "and that big, scruffy one looks like ... a bugbear." The thought made her grin. Before she and her parents had moved into Willow Cottage, she had never heard of flutterpuffs or bugbears! But over the summer, she and Kat had helped out at Calico Comfrey's Veterinary Surgery, taking care of all sorts of curious creatures. She couldn't wait for the weekend so she and Kat could go into the magical forest again.

Suddenly, there was a flash of scarlet in the corner of the playground as a bright red bird took off from a tree. He left a sparkling trail of light behind him as he soared into the sky. Rosie stared in astonishment. Surely this was a magical creature of some sort? But that was impossible! The magical animals hardly ever left the safety of Starfall Forest.

Just then, Miss Lavender clapped her hands to get everyone's attention. "Now I want to talk about the school council," she said. Rosie turned her attention to the teacher. "Every class has one student on the council," continued Miss Lavender. "They meet once a week to discuss important matters."

A girl with curly, red hair put up her hand. "What sort of matters?" she asked.

"They talk about everything from lunches to recycling," smiled Miss Lavender, "and of course, they help to plan events like next week's school fundraiser."

Rosie knew all about the fundraiser. There was going to be a musical show and a bake sale after school on Monday. Her mother had promised to make mini cheesecakes!

"So, do I have any volunteers?" asked Miss Lavender.

Rosie put up her hand eagerly—but so did everyone else! She stretched her hand as high as she could, and wiggled her fingers, as the teacher looked around the classroom.

"Thank you, Luca," said Miss Lavender. "You can represent our class on the council this year."

Rosie put down her hand, feeling sad. She would have loved to be on the school council! She enjoyed taking on responsibilities. And now that she was helping at Calico Comfrey's, she felt quite grown up. Apart from Kat, none of the other kids knew anything about taking care of the Starfall animals.

The bell rang for the lunchtime break and everyone jumped to their feet, calling to each other as they scrambled for the door. Rosie stood up slowly. She didn't know many of their names yet.

"Rosie!" sang a friendly voice behind her.

Rosie let out a sigh of relief. "Hi, Kat!"

Her best friend was hopping from foot to foot, her curly black ponytail bouncing. She took Rosie's hand and gave it a squeeze.

"Let's go out and play!" she said.

Rosie was so glad she had met Kat at the start of the summer. Kat lived in Springhaven with her parents, her twin brothers Jordan and Jayden, and her baby sister Brianna—as well as six chickens, four hamsters, two cats, and an iguana. Together, the two girls had explored Starfall and met the vets. Kat had never ventured into Starfall Forest before, so they had discovered its magic together.

"Hey, Maisie! What shall we play?" shouted Kat, as she tried to pull Rosie into the middle of the schoolyard.

Rosie hung back. She wasn't sure who Maisie was. Everyone seemed to be shouting and running around. What she *really* wanted to do was sit on a bench and talk quietly to Kat about the bright red bird she had seen through the classroom window.

"Let's play Never Wake a Gem Dragon," called someone.

Rosie saw that it was Luca—the boy who was on the school council. "How does *he* know about gem dragons?" she muttered.

Gem dragons lived in the Crystal Caves deep in the heart of Starfall Forest. There was an enchantment on the forest that meant most people never even thought about entering it. It was only thanks to the magic of Rosie's home—Willow Cottage—that the spell didn't work on her and Kat.

"He doesn't," giggled Kat. "Kids here know the names of lots of magical creatures, but everyone thinks they're just stories."

"Oh, I see," said Rosie. "Well, if he'd ever met a gem dragon—like *we* have—he'd know that it's okay to wake them, because they're very friendly."

Kat wasn't really listening. She jogged up and down on the spot, eager to get into the game. "C'mon, Rosie, let's play!" she said.

The children formed a circle around Luca, who closed his eyes and started to count.

"Luca's the gem dragon," explained Kat. "We have to creep up and tap him on the shoulder—but if he opens his eyes, we all scatter before he can catch us."

"You play," said Rosie. "I'll watch."

"I'll be back in a minute," Kat promised.

Suddenly, Rosie heard a faint buzzing noise coming from her pocket. She turned away from the other children and took out the crystalzoometer the vets had given her. From the outside, it looked like an ordinary, heart-shaped locket. Yet hidden inside was a crystal that buzzed whenever a magical animal was near.

Now, the crystal was glowing with a milky light, and its tip pointed to the edge of the schoolyard, where the trees of Starfall leaned over the fence. None of the other children noticed as Rosie crossed the yard, the crystal quivering and glowing brighter with every step she took.

Rosie had almost reached the fence before she saw it. Sitting on the branch of a tree was a baby grumpling covered in soft brown fur, with cornflower-blue stripes around its tail.

The little creature was fast asleep, sucking its thumb and twitching its long fluffy tail as it dreamed. What was this baby doing so far from Grumpling Grove? And why was it all alone? Baby grumplings needed a lot of looking after! They usually rode on their parents' backs, clinging to their fur—but this baby looked as if it could tumble out of the tree at any moment!

With every suck on its thumb, it swayed backward, then forward again.

"Wake up, little one," Rosie whispered.

The baby opened its wide, blue eyes and used its tail to give its nose a scratch.

Rosie raced across the schoolyard. "Kat!" she called. "Come and see what I've found!"

At the sound of Rosie's voice, Kat ran toward her … but so did all the other children she was playing with! Before Rosie knew it, they were *all* following her across the yard.

"What is it? What have you found?" everyone asked excitedly. Rosie pointed up into the tree—but the grumpling had gone!

"There's nothing there," said the girl with curly, red hair.

"It's just a tree," grumbled Luca.

Rosie felt her cheeks flush with embarrassment. Everyone must think she was so silly. Before she had a chance to explain, they were all walking away.

"Kat," she whispered. "It was a baby grumpling all on its own."

"We'll go and tell the vets tomorrow," Kat said. "Come and play."

"I don't want to," snapped Rosie. "It's babyish." As soon as the words had left her mouth, Rosie was sorry she'd been rude. But Kat hadn't heard her. She was already running back to the game.

Chapter 2
Into the Woods

"**W**hat *is* that funny smell?" Rosie asked herself. It smelled like ... What was it? Sweet bananas, creamy cheese, and something else. Burned toast?

It was Saturday morning and Rosie was tidying her bedroom before Kat came over. She folded her pajamas, straightened her pillows, then placed Duffy the fluffy duck on top. She had slept with her toy duck since she was very little.

She gave Duffy a stroke on his head, where the fluff was wearing thin, then bounded down the stairs and into the kitchen.

She saw the problem right away. Her mother had started baking for the school fundraiser. She had a smear of mashed banana across her cheek and her hair was white with flour.

"Hi, sweetie," said Mama. "I'm making mini banana cheesecakes."

Among the blobs of butter, spilled sugar, and cracked eggshells was a tray of burned, gently smoking cheesecakes.

A ball of purple fluff floated by in the hot kitchen air. Rosie watched as it landed on the tip of her mother's nose. Mama brushed it away, but it was too late. Her eyes narrowed and her mouth opened. "Aaah-aah-aah ... Achoo!"

Mama blew her nose, sending purple fluff flying. "Where does all this stuff come from?" she groaned, pointing at the floor, where balls of purple and yellow fluff wafted around.

Rosie knew exactly where it came from. At night, when everyone was in bed, some of the flutterpuffs that lived in Starfall Forest climbed in through the catflap. They liked to scratch their backs against the legs of the kitchen table, sending fluffy wool in all directions. When Rosie told her parents this, they just laughed.

"Can I help you bake?" Rosie asked.

Mama shook her head, trying to wipe the banana off her cheek. "I've got a lot to do, and this first batch is a disaster," she said. "It's probably quicker if I do it myself. Why don't you go outside and play?"

Rosie wrinkled up her nose. She didn't want to go outside, she wanted to help! But just then, a strange warbling noise came from the next room.

"Sounds like Dad's rehearsing his performance for the musical show at the fundraiser," said Mama, with a smile.

Rosie went to look and found Dad dancing around the living room, wearing a white suit and sunglasses and holding a wooden spoon.

"Uh-huh-huh!" he grunted into the spoon. "Hello, pumpkin! Do I look like Elvis?" He shook his hips and swung his arms wildly, accidentally catching his fingers in a sparkly spiderweb that dangled from the ceiling.

"Ugh," he groaned, wiping his hand on his suit. "No matter how often I dust, this room is always full of funny-looking spiderwebs. I'm sure that one was heart-shaped!"

Rosie smiled. The spiders in Willow Cottage were not ordinary spiders. Nothing about Willow Cottage was ordinary! Before Rosie and her parents had moved in, the cottage had been owned by one of the vets, Doctor Hart. It was her grandfather, the wizard Calico Comfrey, who had opened the veterinary surgery a hundred years ago.

"Are you ready for the show?" Rosie asked, changing the subject.

"Not really," Dad admitted, sadly. "I keep forgetting the words to the songs."

"I can help," said Rosie. "Miss Lavender taught us a really great way to remember things in class yesterday."

"No thanks, pumpkin," said Dad. "Don't you worry. You've had a tough week, starting at a new school. Go and play!"

Now Dad was telling her to get out from under his feet, too! Why wouldn't anyone take her seriously or let her help?

Slowly, Rosie went up the stairs to her bedroom, and shut the door softly behind her. She curled up on her bed, hugging her knees. The toads on the wallpaper stared at her sympathetically. When Rosie had first moved into Willow Cottage, she'd hated the toad-patterned wallpaper in her new room. Mama had even helped her cover it with pink paint, but however many coats of paint they used, the toads kept reappearing. Now, Rosie rather liked them. They reminded her of the magical vets, and—perhaps—they were even a little bit magical too.

Rosie sighed. Everyone at the *surgery* knew how responsible and helpful she was! Why couldn't her parents or Miss Lavender see it?

She picked up Duffy the fluffy duck and stroked him. And then she had a thought. It was hardly surprising that her parents treated her like a kid ... when her room was full of stuffed toys!

Rosie pulled a large bag out of her closet. Then she threw open her toy chest and tipped everyone out. There was Ella the elephant with the missing eye, Mo Monkey who liked to play dress-up, and Mr. Hopworth the bunny, who was always so soft and squidgy. She put them in the bag. She knelt down to peer under the wardrobe and found Cuddles the cat, Tiny Teddy, and raggedy little Piggywink. They went in too. Finally,

she turned to the bed. She knew she had to do it. Duffy the fluffy duck must go as well. She gave him a kiss on his worn old head, then put him gently in the bag.

"Rosie? What are you doing?"

Rosie had been so busy, she hadn't heard Kat come in. "Hi, Kat." She gave her friend a hug. "I'm sorting out all my old toys. I don't need them anymore."

"But why?" gasped Kat. "Don't you still play with them?"

"I'm too old for them now!" said Rosie. She caught sight of Duffy's fluffy head. She pushed him deeper into the bag.

Kat clasped her hands together. "I don't know when I'll be ready to say goodbye to Big Ted and all my other toys ... I'm definitely not ready yet. Are you sure you're ready? Won't you miss them?"

Rosie sighed. "I've grown up so much this summer. Moving here, working with the vets ..." Duffy was peeking out again. She pushed him down and closed the bag. She sank onto the bed, her shoulders drooping.

Kat looked thoughtfully at her friend, then sat next to her. "Hey, listen to this," she said. "You won't believe what happened to Jordan and Jayden last night."

"What?" asked Rosie, cheering up. The twins were always doing something crazy.

"Well," said Kat, giggling already, "they had hiccups, and nothing could make it stop. Dad gave them some water, which helped for a while, but soon they were hiccuping more than ever. They even tried scaring each other by pulling funny faces—like this."

Kat made a crazy face and Rosie laughed. "Did it work?" she asked.

"Not really," said Kat with a grin. "So Jayden decided to hide behind the sofa and jump out at Jordan ... But he bumped into the table and a huge pile of books fell onto the carpet. It made the loudest crash you've ever heard!"

"Oh no," gasped Rosie.

"He was fine," said Kat. "The funny thing was that the noise gave them such a shock, their hiccups disappeared immediately!"

The girls went down to the kitchen, where Mama was putting another tray of mini banana cheesecakes in the oven. Kat stared in astonishment at the state of the kitchen.

"Can we go outside, Mama?" asked Rosie.

"Sure, sweetie," said Mama. She offered the tray of burned cheesecakes to Kat. "Would you like a cheesecake to take with you?"

"Er ..." started Kat nervously.

"Not right now, thanks," said Rosie, quickly coming to her friend's rescue. "See you later!"

Rosie and Kat made their way down the garden path, keeping their arms away from the thorny bushes that tangled on both sides.

A groak hopped out onto the path in front of them. It looked rather like a toad, but its skin was purple and velvety. The groak wiggled its bright pink horns and trumpeted.

Hooonnnnkkkk!

Rosie winced. The groaks' loud, tuba-like calls often kept her awake at night. As the girls carefully stepped over it, the groak stuck out its long tongue and licked Kat's ankle.

"That tickles!" she laughed.

At the end of the path was the gate that led to Starfall Forest. Rosie called it the Toad Gate, because its rusty iron frame was decorated with the face of a toad.

It was cooler in the forest. The sun shone through the trees, making rippling shadow patterns on the ground, and the leaves rustled in the gentle breeze.

Suddenly, Kat grabbed Rosie's arm. "Listen! What's that?"

Rosie stopped walking. She could hear a soft, sweet sound that rose higher and higher, then fell to a murmur. At the same time, she felt her crystalzoometer whirr to life. For a moment, the air was quiet, then the singing cry rang out again. It was strange and lovely all at once.

"There!" said Rosie, pointing to the top of a tall tree. A red bird flew into the air, his long scarlet tail feathers streaking behind him. Was this the bird that Rosie had seen in the school yard? He certainly looked the same. He was the most gorgeous creature that she had

ever seen—red like a flame, with flashes of orange as he flapped his wings.

"Wow!" said Kat. "What was *that*?" She was examining the branch where the bird had been sitting. Its twigs were blackened and smoking. They smelled a bit like the burned cheesecakes!

Pttttht ... Sssshwt ...

Rosie looked down at her feet and saw a tiny baby groak.

"Awwwww!" said Rosie. "It wants to trumpet like a grown-up but can't manage it yet."

The groak tried again: *Pthshshshswt*. The little creature was trying so hard, it sprayed Rosie with spit.

"Yuck!" she said, wiping her arm.

Kat giggled. She put on a funny, squeaky voice and pretended to be the groak. "Don't be mad at me, Rosie, I'm only a baby!"

Rosie laughed. "I'm not mad—just a bit damp!" she said, stroking the little groak's lilac head. "But, Kat, baby groaks are born in the spring. It's September now, so why is this one still so small?"

Kat shook her head. "I don't know."

"I wonder if it has something to do with the red bird," said Rosie thoughtfully. "This is the second time I've seen him just before finding a baby animal."

Hoooonnnnkkkk! Hoooonnnnkkkk!

An adult groak hopped out from under a bush, followed by two more.

The baby groak bounced up and down with delight, then the four groaks jumped away together.

"Don't worry," said Kat. "Let's go to the surgery and tell Doctor Hart. I bet she'll know what's going on."

Chapter 3
Sleepy Flutterpuffs

Kat and Rosie had just reached the old tree that led to the surgery when they heard a creaky voice coming from somewhere in the leaves high above them.

"Oh dear, oh dear, oh dear ..."

The girls stopped in surprise.

"Quibble?" said Rosie slowly. "Is that you?"

"Of course it's me," came the voice. "I'm up in the tree!"

The girls looked up and saw their friend Quibble, the porter at the surgery. He was always hard to spot among the trees, because he looked just like a small tree stump. His

bark was bristling with the effort of clinging to a wobbling ladder.

"But what are you doing up there?" Rosie asked, looking puzzled.

Quibble pointed at some pink and orange fluffy balls that were dangling from a branch. "The flutterpuffs need help," he said. As he spoke, a strip of moss above his mouth—his moss-tache—jiggled in a worried manner.

"Why, Quibble?" asked Kat. "What's the matter?"

Quibble ran his twiggy hands through the sprouts growing from the top of his stump. "The flutterpuffs are falling asleep when they should be weaving cocoons," he said in a disapproving voice, huffing and puffing as he climbed down the ladder.

Rosie could see lots of flutterpuffs in the tree. The little creatures looked like bright pom-poms dangling from the branches on fluffy threads. Some were spinning the fluff

into striped balls around themselves, but others were just dangling, fast asleep, from the end of their threads. The dozing flutterpuffs swung in the breeze, their cocoons half-finished. Shreds of fluff floated through the air all around them.

"I didn't know they made cocoons," said Rosie. "What happens when they're inside?"

"I bet they change completely," said Kat with excitement. "Like caterpillars when they turn into butterflies. The flutterpuffs must know it's time for them to grow up!"

"Perhaps," muttered Quibble, giving a sudden huge yawn. "But first we must stop them from sleeping on the job. They are making slumberfluff to help them sleep inside their cocoons. But this fluff is so, so, so powerful!" He yawned again and rubbed his eyes with a twiggy finger.

"Slumberfluff for flutterpuffs?" whispered Kat. "Try saying that five times fast!"

Rosie tried, and it made her giggle.

Quibble yawned, his moss-tache twitching. "I must keep them awake," he muttered. But his eyes started closing and he began to topple gently over. "But first, I need a rest …"

"Quibble?" said Kat, bending over him.

Quibble's bark was rising and falling gently. With every breath, he gave a whistling creak.

"He's asleep!" said Rosie.

"I guess the sleepiness is catching!" said Kat, wafting away a shred of slumberfluff.

"Let's let him nap," said Rosie. "We can keep these flutterpuffs awake so they can finish their cocoons. You take this branch and I'll take that one."

Kat stroked the nearest snoozing ball. "Wakey wakey, little flutterpuff." The creature squeaked, opened its eyes, and went back to work. Right away, Kat saw that another flutterpuff had fallen asleep. She dashed over and tickled it. Then she saw another one sleeping at the other end of the branch and ran to wake it, too.

Rosie decided to form a plan. Starting at one end of her branch, she worked her way along, gently tapping each flutterpuff in turn. When she reached the end of the branch, she started again at the beginning.

"That's a good system," said Kat.

"Yes, but you're doing just as well as I am," laughed Rosie, waving a shred of fluff out of her face. "Look, all your flutterpuffs are awake and finishing their cocoons."

It was true—the cocoons on both Kat's and Rosie's branches were nearly finished. In a few more minutes, there were no more flutterpuffs to be seen. Every single one was now woven snugly inside a flutterpuff slumberfluff pouch.

"Now there's one more creature to wake up," giggled Kat. She bent down and gave Quibble a little pat on the head.

"Eh?" spluttered Quibble, sitting upright. Then he saw the cocoons were all finished. "Oh, well done, well done, well done!"

"I can't wait to see what the flutterpuffs look like when they come out," said Rosie.

Quibble started to pick up the leftover slumberfluff that was drifting along the ground. "Yes," he said. "But now we must collect this fluff before it sends the whole forest to sleep." The girls joined in, filling their pockets with soft fluff.

"Time to come inside," said Quibble. With a twiggy hand, he pressed on the wide trunk of the large oak tree that led to the surgery.

Chapter 4
A Strange Visitor

"*C*ome along, come along," said Quibble. Rosie and Kat followed Quibble inside. The door in the tree gently closed behind them, and Rosie felt for Kat's hand. After a moment, her eyes got used to the darkness, and she could see the spiral staircase winding its way downward in the gloom.

As they followed Quibble down and around, they noticed a golden glow at the bottom of the stairs. Hundreds of tiny, shiny beetles were fluttering about on the wall.

"Lampbugs!" sighed Quibble. "Dear me, they get everywhere."

Rosie secretly thought they were lovely! They walked past the glowing bugs and read the sign beside the surgery door:

CALICO COMFREY'S VETERINARY SURGERY

Welcome one and welcome all,
Magical creatures of Starfall!
Dragon, toad, or unicorn,
With injured tooth, or paw, or horn,
Come inside—this magic's real—
Our team of vets is here to heal!

The door was, in fact, not one door but four, each door set inside a door a little bigger than itself.

Quibble unlocked the smallest door and walked through. Of course, the girls could not follow him, and waited patiently for him to open one of the larger doors. Quibble peered around the smallest door and said,

"What are you waiting for? Come in, come in, come in!"

"Um, would you mind opening a bigger door, please, Quibble?" asked Kat.

"What am I thinking?" tutted Quibble. "I always forget how huge Normilliams are!"

At once, the largest door swung open and the girls stepped into the surgery.

Rosie gasped. The room was filled with animals of all shapes and sizes, running, bouncing, and scuttling. The noise of mewing, sneezing, and giggling was deafening.

Doctor Hart was standing in the middle of it all, holding a struggling kitten-like creature that was trying to use its little wings to fly away. Her flowery hat had nearly been knocked off her head, but when she saw the girls, her round face broke into a smile. "Hello, dearies! I'll be with you in a minute."

Rosie scanned the chaotic scene and saw Doctor Morel balancing on a stool, grasping a handkerchief and reaching for an owl-like creature that was perched on a stump.

"Toadstools and trinkets!" he gasped. "Come along now, you crazy cahoot."

Like most gnomes, Doctor Morel was not very tall. He had a long beard and wore a green pointed hat, from which a crop of mushrooms was growing.

"Achoo!" sneezed the cahoot, bobbing up and down like a beach ball.

As Doctor Morel stretched toward the sniffling cahoot, teetering on his tiptoes, another one sprang off the wall and flew into the poor vet, knocking him over!

"Twitty-woo," it sang cheerfully.

The girls rushed over. "Are you all right, Doctor Morel?" asked Kat.

"Too busy to talk," said Doctor Morel grumpily, getting up and turning back to the cahoots. "This flock of cahoots got very cold playing on the frozen lake yesterday, and now they've all got runny beaks. They really *must* be encouraged to blow them into these handkerchiefs. If they don't, their feathers will start to freeze. Before we know it, they'll all be owlcicles!"

"Can we help, Doctor Morel?" asked Kat.

Tingaling! The vet was about to answer when a bell rang from the noticeboard on the wall. On it, the words *Blow the cahoots' noses* faded and were replaced by a new instruction: *Trim the smittens' claws.*

"I *am* trying," sighed Doctor Hart, waving a hand at the magical noticeboard. Her eyes crinkled as she smiled at the girls. "These poor smittens have got the awful clawfuls! Their claws just won't stop growing. I've given them medicine, but it takes a while to work. In the meantime, they need their claws clipped so they don't get sore whenever they have a scratch. However ..." She pulled clippers from her apron pocket. "They do not like having their claws trimmed one bit."

The little pink smitten she was holding offered her its left front paw, hiding its right paw behind its back.

"Oh you silly smitten!" said Doctor Hart. "I've trimmed that one already. Show me the other one."

With a small mew, the smitten leapt from her arms and fluttered back to its friends.

"Oh dear," sighed Doctor Hart. "All the smittens look alike, so it is very hard to keep track of which ones have been clipped."

"Can we help you catch them?" asked Rosie. She really wanted to help out—and show how useful she could be.

"Oh my kettles and cuttlefish!" cried Doctor Morel. He had been knocked over again and a playful cahoot was jumping up and down on his back.

Tingaling-tingaling-tingaling! It was the magic noticeboard. Now it said: *Tidy up the chamedeons' patterns.*

"What's a cam ... cham ... chamedeon?" asked Rosie, looking around. She'd heard of cham*eleons*. They were able to change their skin shade to match their surroundings Perhaps these creatures were similar?

Doctor Hart was searching the room with a smitten tucked under each arm. "There they are," she said, pointing to a group of giggling lizards hiding under a bench.

"Oh!" giggled Rosie. These creatures didn't blend in at all. As she watched, their skins changed from red and purple spots to yellow

and green stripes. This made them laugh so much that they fell over!

"They have a bad case of clashitis," explained Doctor Hart. "Their skin won't stop changing to crazy patterns. It makes them giggle so much that—well—the patterns just fall off!" Doctor Hart waved a hand and the girls saw that the floor was covered in all sorts of bright spots and stripes. "Don't worry, my dearies, it doesn't hurt them at all—but it makes a terrible mess."

"I'll help," said Rosie at once. "Where's the broom?"

"Over in the corner," replied Doctor Hart.

Rosie ran to fetch the broom, but as she was bringing it back, a cahoot sprang off the ceiling and knocked into her, sending the broom flying out of her hand!

"Are you all right?" asked Doctor Hart, rushing over and rubbing Rosie's arm.

"Oh yes, thank you," said Rosie.

"I'd better take this," said Doctor Hart, picking up the broom with a kind smile.

"I really want to help," Rosie said quietly to Kat. "*You* know I'm grown up enough to sweep, and clip, and blow noses."

"Of course you are," said Kat, giving her a hug. "You're so organized. Not like me! I'm always losing my sneakers and forgetting my homework and … Look out!"

A boombadger had wandered into the room. It looked a bit like a badger, but its fur was a patchwork of green squares. The boombadger looked around the room and sniffed the air. Suddenly all its fur stood straight out on end ...

"Run!" yelled Rosie.

Everyone—the girls, the vets, Quibble, even the other animals—rushed to get as far from the boombadger as possible.

There was a very loud BOOO-OOM! and the room filled with a terrible smell.

Kat flapped her hands in front of her face. "I never know whether to put my hands over my ears or my nose," she groaned.

"Silly boombadger," said Quibble, wagging a twiggy finger. The boombadger snuffled happily.

The chamedeons found the boombadger even funnier than their clashitis. The more they laughed, the more their dots and spots fell off, so Doctor Hart had to go straight back to work with her broom.

Suddenly, Rosie saw that, while everyone was distracted, a visitor had arrived at the surgery. A gnome, wearing a large, shiny helmet, was waiting by the door, impatiently tapping his feet on the floor. He looked very old indeed, with a face covered in crisscrossing wrinkles and a white beard so long that it touched his toes. He was holding a tiny foal on a leash.

Rosie decided to go over and see if she could help.

"Hi," she said. "I'm Rosie."

"And I," said the gnome, pushing out his chest proudly, "am Sir Horatio Hornswaggle, Knight of the Order of the Green Garter."

Rosie picked up a notebook and pencil. "I'm afraid the vets are busy right now, but perhaps I could write down your problem?"

Sir Horatio looked surprised. "I don't know how you can help *me*—Sir Horatio Hornswaggle," he said. "I'll wait to talk to a real vet, if you don't mind."

Rosie gasped, and Kat reached out and gave her hand a sympathetic squeeze.

Unlike its owner, the little foal was very friendly. It nuzzled against Rosie's leg, hoping for a treat. Kat sat down to cuddle it. She stroked its silky mane and its soft, smooth back.

Then Doctor Morel came over holding a squirming cahoot.

"Greetings," said the gnome grandly. "I am Sir Horatio Hornswaggle! Knight of the Order of the—"

"Yes, yes," said Doctor Morel, while struggling with the cahoot. "Is your foal sick?"

"Oh no, Humphrey is quite well," said Sir Horatio. "But until a short time ago, he was a full-grown horse. Now—very suddenly—he's a foal again. What are you going to do about it?"

Kat nudged Rosie like she always did when she'd thought of a joke. "Maybe he needs some throat medicine," she suggested.

"Why?" barked Sir Horatio.

"Because he's a little horse!"

Rosie broke into giggles and Doctor Morel swallowed a chuckle.

Sir Horatio frowned and shook his beard. "This is no laughing matter," he grumbled.

Then Rosie gave a little gasp. "Doctor Morel!" she said. "We had something to tell you, but you've all been so busy that we forgot! There's a strange red bird in the forest—and we've seen other baby animals that are young when they just shouldn't be."

"Oh my spoons and jars!" said Doctor Morel. "That sounds like phoenix magic." He turned to the old gnome. "Did *you* spot any red birds before your horse changed?"

Sir Horatio looked a little embarrassed. "Yes I ... ummm ... I think I did ... spot a phoenix shortly before it happened. I should have ... er ... mentioned it."

"A phoenix has very powerful magic," explained Doctor Morel gravely. "Every morning, a phoenix hatches from its own egg. Over the course of the day, it grows up. And by bedtime, it is really quite old.

So, every night, before it goes to sleep, it turns back into an egg, ready for the new day. But something has gone wrong if the phoenix's magic is affecting other creatures like this." He patted Humphrey, and the foal gave a happy snort. "Something very strange must have happened to this phoenix ... Something very strange indeed."

Chapter 5
Off to Grumpling Grove

"This is an emergency, girls," said Doctor Morel. "This phoenix must be found before any more damage is done."

"We can start searching right away," said Rosie eagerly.

Doctor Morel nodded and turned to Sir Horatio, whose helmet seemed to have slammed shut. "Hello?" he called. There was no answer from inside the helmet. "Sir Horatio?" he called again, louder. "Fuss and fiddlesticks! Where were you when your horse ... er ... shrank?"

"Wait a moment!" There was a creak as the old knight pulled open his helmet and peered out at them again. "In Grumpling Grove," he said eventually, giving his beard a bad-tempered twirl.

Doctor Hart bustled forward. "Why don't you show Doctor Morel and the girls the exact spot, Sir Horatio?" she suggested. "I'm sure Doctor Clarice can take you all there. Don't worry—I'll look after Humphrey."

Rosie and Kat followed Doctor Morel down the twisting, earthy corridor that led to Doctor Clarice's laboratory. Sir Horatio hurried along behind them, bumping into the walls every now and then as he struggled to keep his helmet open.

Doctor Clarice was the third of the surgery's vets. She was also a very clever inventor and her lab was packed with tools, tubes, and

gadgets. Flasks bubbled, buttons flashed, and wheels whirred whenever she was working on a new experiment. Rosie had noticed that she always had a pencil stuck behind one ear so she could make notes whenever a new idea popped into her head.

"Kat! Rosie! I can't wait to show you my latest invention," cried Doctor Clarice, excitedly brushing her long, red hair out of her eyes. "The bubblerunners gave me an idea for a new vehicle. It's such fun—and it goes really fast!"

Bubblerunners? Rosie thought. Then she noticed the sparkling bubbles that were floating around the room. Inside each one was a fluffy, hamster-like animal, running around and around. The little creatures were chattering noisily as they made the bubbles spin higher and lower, left and right.

"Fast, you say?" said Doctor Morel. "Well, we need to get to Grumpling Grove as fast as possible. A phoenix needs our help."

"Perfect!" said Doctor Clarice, her eyes lighting up behind her glasses. "Let's get the Bubblemobile started."

Doctor Clarice told everyone to squeeze onto a small bench. Then, she pressed a button on its base. There was a rumbling noise, and a glass tube slid out from the side of the bench, winding up and back and around. A funnel popped out of the end and a stream of little strawberry-pink bubbles flew out into the room.

"Doctor Clarice!" said Doctor Morel, gripping the bench in alarm. "Are you sure this is safe?"

"Oh yes," said Doctor Clarice, calmly. "Quite sure. I've run lots of tests."

Rosie and Kat looked at each other nervously. The bench was shaking so hard that Rosie's teeth chattered. Bubbles popped up the tube and out of the funnel ...

"Perhaps we should walk to Grumpling Grove," suggested Sir Horatio.

But it was too late! The funnel had blown one huge, pink bubble that was stretching itself around the bench. First Sir Horatio, then Doctor Morel, Doctor Clarice, and the girls all found themselves inside it!

"It smells like candy," giggled Kat.

With one last rumble, the tube folded itself away, and the bubble lifted up into the air, carrying the bench—and its passengers— out of the laboratory and into the forest. Bouncing off branches and brushing against leaves, it floated higher and higher until they could look right down on the treetops.

"It's amazing!" cried Kat.

"I'm glad you like it," said Doctor Clarice, setting the controls for Grumpling Grove.

Off they flew, bobbing over the trees at a startling pace. They sped over the Mazewood, where Rosie looked down and glimpsed a family of fox-like kitsunes tumbling over each other as they chased each other's tails. It seemed like lots of fun, especially as kitsunes have three tails each.

Then the Bubblemobile bounced over the Lollipop Orchard, where a noisy flock of twocans were licking at the lollipops that grew from the trees. Startled by the sight of the huge bubble, a pair flew up to take a look. Twocans are strange birds that can only fly in twos. They each wrap one wing around the other and use the other wing to flap!

"I can see Grumpling Grove," said Kat, as the Bubblemobile started to sink down between the trees, squeezing its way through the leaves and branches.

The Bubblemobile landed in Grumpling Grove, and the bubble burst with a giant POP!

"Don't worry, that's perfectly normal," said Doctor Clarice.

Everyone stood up, then jumped in surprise as the bench shivered and threw out a shower of sparks.

"Oops! That's not," said Doctor Clarice. "I think the oscillating discombobulator sprocket's come loose." She pulled her spare toolkit out of her pocket. "No problem. It will only take me a moment to fix."

As she got to work, a group of grumplings bounded over to meet them. They sprang up and down, using their long curly tails like springs and chuckling happily.

"I don't see why they're called grumplings," said Rosie. "They're not grumpy at all!"

"It's a funny story," said Doctor Morel. "When Calico Comfrey discovered Starfall, he met a very grumpy grumpling—so he assumed that all grumplings were grumpy!"

"But they're so cute," giggled Kat.

"Aren't we here to find the phoenix?" grumbled Sir Horatio.

Rosie sighed. If Sir Horatio had been the first gnome she'd met, she might have assumed that all *gnomes* were grumpy! It was lucky she'd met other gnomes before him.

Chapter 6
In Search of the Phoenix

Rosie's crystalzoometer buzzed in her pocket. There must be an animal in trouble nearby. Perhaps it was the phoenix!

She opened the magical gadget and saw that the crystal was spinning around quickly. First it was pointing to the left ... then straight ahead ... then to the right! The grumplings sprang up and down beside her as they tried to see the sparkling crystal.

"Careful they don't break your zoometer, Rosie," warned Doctor Morel. "Sometimes grumplings can be *too* bouncy!"

"Never mind all that," said Sir Horatio impatiently. "Off we go!"

They left Doctor Clarice tinkering with the Bubblemobile and set off through the trees, following the direction the zoometer was pointing. The problem was it never stayed pointing in the same direction for long.

"Fennel and fiddlesticks!" exclaimed Doctor Morel. "It feels like we're walking in circles." He checked his own crystalzoometer, but it was doing exactly the same thing.

"I'm not a young gnome," complained Sir Horatio. "All this walking is making my back ache, you know."

Rosie's crystal swung from left to right.

"There," cried Kat. "It's in that tree!"

But as soon as they approached the tree, it lifted its roots out of the ground and started to run away! Gold and green flames flickered around the tree's branches.

"Follow that tree!" shouted Sir Horatio. The group gave chase. By the time the tree stopped again, they were all out of breath.

"It's one of the trees from the Wandering Woods," puffed Rosie. "No wonder the crystal kept moving around!"

"Is the phoenix burning its branches?" asked Kat anxiously.

"Oh no," said Doctor Morel. "Phoenix fire would never harm a living tree."

The wandering tree came to a stop a little distance away.

"I am a Knight of the Green Garter," said Sir Horatio crossly, "and I order you to sit!"

The tree did not like being spoken to in that tone one bit! It rustled its leaves in annoyance, and Kat rolled her eyes at the bad-tempered knight.

"Let me try," Rosie said quickly. She tiptoed forward and gently patted the tree's trunk. "Hello wandering tree," she said sweetly. "I'm very pleased to meet you."

The tree gave its leaves a happy shake and sat down on the grass beside her with a loud creak.

"Well done, Rosie," cheered Kat.

"Yes, yes, very good," said Doctor Morel.

"No time to waste," barked Sir Horatio. "This bird must come down."

"We could climb up to get him," suggested Kat.

"Impossible!" Sir Horatio roared, shaking his head so hard that his helmet slammed shut. "Have you never heard of the old gnome saying?" he added in a muffled voice. "*A wise gnome's feet never leave the street.*"

"What does that mean?" asked Rosie.

"I think gnomes are afraid of heights," whispered Kat.

"Anyway, it's easy to bring the bird down to us," said Sir Horatio. "I'm sure he would like a nice, juicy pepperpear. I have the finest crop of them in my garden in Gnome Town."

To Rosie's astonishment, the gnome reached under his helmet and pulled out a knobbly, green fruit.

At once, there was a rustling in the branches, and the red, feathery head of the phoenix peeked down at them. At first, he gave an excited chirrup at the sight of the pepperpear—then the effort of moving seemed to be too much. He closed his eyes and lay down on the branch.

"Goodness me!" tutted Doctor Morel. "I don't think he's well enough to fly."

Just then, a grumpling jumped through the trees toward them, chuckling excitedly. It sprang around the girls, then bounced up the trunk of the wandering tree.

The phoenix opened his eyes to see what all the noise was about—and there was a sudden flash of flickering green flames as he gave an immense HICCUP!

"Oh no!" cried Rosie. But it was too late. The grumpling that bounced back down the tree was now a baby, half the size it had been a moment before. The tiny grumpling put its thumb in its mouth and started to suck. Rosie rushed to pick it up and it snuggled into her arms.

"Cymbals and celery!" said Doctor Morel in surprise. "That bird's got magiccups."

"Is that magic hiccups?" said Kat.

"Can they be cured?" asked Rosie.

"Perhaps," said Doctor Morel. "But first we need to bring the poor bird down."

"I'll do it," said Kat. "I don't mind heights."

"What if the phoenix hiccups when you're up there?" said Rosie in a worried voice. "You might turn into a toddler!"

Doctor Morel pulled a glittering blanket out of his bag. "When you reach the phoenix, wrap him in this special blanket," he said. "It will stop the magic from changing you."

"Shall I climb up with you?" asked Rosie. She wasn't sure that she wanted to—but she couldn't let her friend go alone.

"No," said Kat. "I'd rather you stayed on the ground and kept talking to this tree! It seems to like you ... and I don't want it to wander off with me in the branches!"

"Very sensible," said Doctor Morel.

Kat looked up at the lowest branch. It was too high for her to reach! She jumped as high as she could and stretched her hand up—but it was no use.

Rosie put down the baby grumpling and patted the tree's rough bark. "Can you help us, please?" she asked in a soft voice.

At once, the tree reached out with one of its branches, the twigs wiggling like fingers. The twigs took Kat's hand and lifted her up into the air!

Kat let out a peal of laughter. "Wow!" she gasped, holding the magic blanket tightly as the tree passed her from branch to branch. "I've never climbed a tree like this before."

Gently, the tree placed Kat down on a wide branch beside the phoenix.

"Thank you, wandering tree," said Rosie, hugging its trunk. "You're the most helpful tree I've ever met! Now please stay very, very still ..."

The phoenix was nestled in a thick clump of leaves at the end of the branch. He gave a tired chirrup and green flames flickered weakly around him. His golden eyes were shut, and he didn't seem to have noticed Kat.

"Use the blanket!" called Rosie, hopping anxiously from one foot to the other.

Very carefully, Kat unfolded the magic blanket and spread it over the little bird.

"Be careful!" warned Doctor Morel.

The phoenix snuggled into the soft blanket,

and Kat gently scooped him up. She held the bird close and stroked his feathery cheek.

"You did it!" called Rosie happily. She gave the wandering tree a gentle pat. "Thank you for standing so still," she whispered.

But Kat was looking worried. "I don't think I can climb down if I'm holding the phoenix," she said.

"What goes up, must come down," Sir Horatio said unhelpfully.

"Don't worry," said Rosie, giving the gnome a hard stare. "I'm sure the tree can lend a hand—I mean branch!" She gave the wandering tree a little hug. "Please could you help us again, tree?"

The tree gave an obliging rustle and wrapped a branch around Kat's waist.

"Oh my moss and mothballs! Hold on tight," called Doctor Morel.

The branch dipped down, carrying Kat and the little bird to safety. It unwound to let Kat go as soon as her feet touched the ground.

"Thank you, wandering tree," said Kat.

The tree shook its leaves and stood up with a loud creak. Then, with a funny little bow, it strode away.

Rosie rushed over to her friend and gave her a hug. "You were amazing!" she said.

"So were you," replied Kat, grinning.

Rosie took hold of the bird. "What shall we call him?" she asked.

"How about ... Blaze!" said Kat.

"That's a good name," said Rosie, stroking the bird's soft feathers. "What do you think, little phoenix?"

The phoenix gave a weak squawk of agreement.

"Let me have a look at the patient," said Doctor Morel, hurrying over. "Oh dear, this isn't good. Not good at all!"

The phoenix's feathers were now more pink than red, and his wingtips were white.

"Blaze is getting old," said Doctor Morel. "His phoenix magic should be keeping him young—but, thanks to the hiccups, it's changing other creatures instead. We need to get him back to the surgery at once."

Chapter 7
The Blanket Thief

HICCUUUUP!

Doctor Morel jumped back in alarm, and Sir Horatio scurried to hide behind the nearest tree. Rosie and Kat stared at each other with wide eyes.

"It's all right," said Doctor Morel, puffing out a huge sigh of relief. "The magic blanket is working. Nobody has turned into a baby. You can come out now, Sir Horatio."

"I was just ... er ... yes ..." mumbled the old gnome. Sheepishly, he came out from behind the tree and the group set off in the direction of the Bubblemobile.

The Blanket Thief

All at once, a grumpling sprang out of the bushes and started to jump alongside them. Before anyone could say a word, it grabbed hold of the magic blanket and tugged it off the little phoenix—whisking it away before Rosie had time to blink!

"Hey!" yelled Rosie. "We need that. Come back!" But it was no use. The grumpling bounced up a tree and out of sight.

"Oh my worms and weevils!" gasped Doctor Morel. "What was that all about?"

"The Normilliam should have held onto the blanket tighter," sniffed Sir Horatio.

"It's not her fault," said Kat hotly.

Rosie was grateful to her friend for sticking up for her. She was starting to get a bit fed up of Sir Horatio's bad-tempered ways, but she had bigger worries on her mind right now. She looked down at the bird cradled in her arms and Blaze looked sleepily back at her. He looked so sweet and harmless—it was hard to believe that just holding him was putting her in danger.

"Blaze could hiccup again at any moment," warned Doctor Morel. "We must get the blanket back."

Blaze gave a tired squawk. The poor thing looked very sorry for himself.

"First, let's give Blaze some water to soothe his throat," Doctor Morel said. "It won't cure the hiccups, but it might give us enough time to find that silly grumpling."

He opened his bag and pulled out a flask of water. Then he poured some into Kat's waiting palms. Blaze lapped up every last drop and gave a happy sigh.

"Sir Horatio and I will take Blaze back to the Bubblemobile," said Doctor Morel. "You two must go and ask the grumpling queen for help."

"Where does she live?" asked Rosie, passing the sleepy little bird to the vet.

"In her Grumpcastle, of course," said Doctor Morel, waving his arms around. "It's right in the middle of Grumpling Grove. You can't miss it."

Rosie and Kat hurried off in the direction the vet had pointed. They walked through the trees, looking left and right as they went, but there was nothing that looked even a bit like a castle.

"What do you think a Grumpcastle actually *looks* like?" asked Kat, eventually.

"Oooh," said Rosie, coming to a stop. She started to giggle. "I think that it looks like a giant sandcastle." She pointed over Kat's shoulder.

Kat swung around to look, and there it was. "It's so cute!" she squealed.

The castle was the same size as a children's playhouse. Its walls were shaped from sun-baked mud, and flags made of twigs and leaves flew from its turrets. The round doorway looked just about wide enough for Rosie and Kat to crawl inside.

"In we go, then," said Rosie, feeling a little nervous. She had never met a queen before. Should she call her "Your Highness" or "Your Majesty?" She didn't think there would be room to curtsey in such a tiny place!

Rosie crawled along the dark, earthy tunnel on her hands and knees, her elbows scraping against the walls. Kat was close behind her.

"Sorry!" Kat said, as she bumped her head against Rosie's bottom.

"That's all right," giggled Rosie.

A loud squeaking filled the girls' ears as they crawled into a round walled room. The grumpling queen was not alone! Lying on the floor, wrapped in the magic blanket, were five baby grumplings.

"Wow, what a noise!" said Kat as she emerged from the tunnel behind Rosie.

The babies were all whining and wriggling, waving their little paws around, poking each other, then squeaking loudly.

"I don't think they're real babies at all," said Rosie. "I think they're grumplings that

have been de-aged by Blaze!" She turned to
the grumpling queen. "Erm ... excuse me,
Your Royal Majesty," she said bravely. "Did
your friends get turned into babies by a
hiccuping phoenix?"

The queen nodded her head up and down
so fast that her flower crown slipped down
over her ears. She pushed it back with a paw.

"She must be so worried," whispered Kat.

"I bet she sent that grumpling to find
something soft for the babies to lie on," replied
Rosie. "That's why he took the blanket!"

"She's probably hoping it will help them take a nap," said Kat. "My baby sister always gets noisy and wriggly when she's tired."

"Well, it's not working," said Rosie. Every time the queen soothed one little grumpling, another one started to wail. Then an idea struck her. "Ooh! But I know what will ..."

Kat looked at her with a puzzled expression.

"The flutterpuffs' slumberfluff," said Rosie, digging her hands into her pocket and bringing out a handful.

"Of course!" said Kat excitedly.

"Your Majesty," said Rosie in a soft voice. "I'm so sorry, but we need to take our magic blanket back. Without it, the phoenix's hiccups could de-age everyone in Starfall. You can use this slumberfluff instead. It's much better—I promise that the babies will be asleep in no time!"

The queen looked at the girls and nodded. Gently, she pulled the blanket away and handed it over. Then Rosie and Kat wrapped the babies snugly in the soft slumberfluff. In a moment, they were all fast asleep, giving little whistling snores. The queen gave a huge—tired—smile.

"Thank you, Your Majesty," whispered Rosie. "Sleep well, baby grumplings."

The girls crawled out of the Grumpcastle and made their way back to the clearing, where Doctor Clarice was standing beside the Bubblemobile.

"It's working again," she called cheerfully.

"That's great," said Kat. "But where's Doctor Morel and Sir Horatio? Where's Blaze?"

"Salmon and soapflakes! Will someone give me a hand?" came a grumbling voice from the trees. The girls turned and saw the strangest sight. Doctor Morel was staggering toward them with Blaze under one arm— and a very young gnome under the other.

"Hello! Who's this little one?" asked Doctor Clarice in surprise.

"Me Howwashio!" said the baby, proudly.

Rosie's mouth dropped open. "Sir Horatio?"

"Blaze must have started hiccuping again," said Kat. "Quick—the blanket!"

She snatched the magic blanket from Rosie's hands and wrapped it around Blaze before he could open his beak.

Doctor Morel sighed in relief. "Back to

the surgery everyone," he said. "Donuts and dandelions, what a day!"

In no time at all, the Bubblemobile had bounced them back to the surgery. Doctor Hart was waiting outside with some very good news. "It seems like the phoenix's magic only lasts for a few hours," she told them. "Humphrey is fully grown again."

"Humpree!" lisped Sir Horatio adorably. His little face glowed at the sight of his horse, and he toddled over and hugged its leg.

Kat and Rosie couldn't stop staring at the little Sir Horatio.

"Will he be okay?" Kat asked.

Doctor Hart smiled. "He'll be fine. I'll just have to keep him out of mischief until the phoenix magic wears off."

"You know ... I kind of like him better as a baby," said Rosie with a grin.

Baby Sir Horatio grabbed at Humphrey's tail and giggled. His horse gave an annoyed snort and swished it out of his reach.

Doctor Hart laughed and scooped up the baby gnome. "He's still a bit of a handful," she said. "Don't worry, we'll keep him safe until he grows back to his usual age. Thank you for all your help today. Blaze is in good hands now, thanks to you."

"We're always happy to help," said Rosie.

Hand in hand, the girls ran home through

the woods. When they reached Rosie's garden, they hugged each other goodbye and made a plan to meet early the next morning.

Rosie found her mother in the kitchen, still hard at work with the cheesecakes.

"Hi, Mama," she said.

"Hi sweetie," smiled her mother. "Did you have fun?"

"Oh yes," said Rosie. "We found a phoenix!"

"That's nice," said Mama.

Rosie grinned. Mama never believed her when she talked about the forest creatures.

"So, how many mini banana cheesecakes have you made?" Rosie asked.

"I was aiming for one hundred, but the mixture ran out after ninety-six," said Mama.

"I bet they're ... er ... delicious," said Rosie, biting her lip as she looked at the unusual treats lined up on the table.

"All they need now is a swirl of chocolate frosting on top to finish them off," Mama said. "Would you like to do it?"

"Yes please!" said Rosie.

Her mother handed her the frosting bag and stroked Rosie's cheek. "Thank you," she said. "I know how much you like to help out, but it's important for you to make time to play, too. When you're older, you'll have nothing but responsibility!"

Rosie nodded. Then, she started to squeeze the gloopy chocolate frosting over the top of a mini cheesecake. It wasn't easy to do. In fact, it was much harder than Rosie had thought. But she didn't want to complain because Mama looked so worn out from all her cooking. In fact ...

Shu-whooooo! Shu-whooooo! Mama was now asleep and gently snoring, Rosie felt tired too, but she was determined to finish decorating the cheesecakes ...

All ninety-six of them!

Chapter 8
Hiccup Havoc

"We're all in here, dearies," called Doctor Hart. "Come in, come in!"

It was Sunday morning and the girls had arrived at the surgery bright and early. Rosie and Kat picked their way through skittering smittens and sneezing cahoots to the examination room.

The three vets were gathered around Blaze, looking very worried. The little bird was lying in a basket, tucked under the magic blanket. He looked so tired that he could barely lift a wing to greet the girls.

"I'm afraid he's been hiccuping all night,"

said Doctor Clarice. "He's exhausted! Luckily, the blanket has kept us all safe."

"Poor Blaze!" gasped Rosie.

Just then, Sir Horatio bustled into the room. He was fully grown again, and his beard looked longer than ever. "I know what will settle his stomach," he said bossily. "A little snack." He reached under his helmet, took out a pepperpear, and held it near Blaze's beak.

"No, no," yelped Doctor Hart. "Phoenixes love pepperpears, but they must never, ever eat them. It gives them an allergic reaction."

It was too late. Blaze had already snapped up the tasty green treat and swallowed it whole.

"Maybe one won't hurt," said Rosie hopefully.

Blaze sat up and gulped. His eyes started to water and steam seeped from his beak.

"It's not just one," groaned Sir Horatio. "I have been feeding Blaze a pepperpear every day to get him down from his tree ..."

"What?" gasped Doctor Hart. "Why?"

"I ... I ... I wanted to be a hundred again," answered the knight. "I'm five hundred, you know! I wanted his magic to work on me." He stared at his feet. "I didn't know it would cause all this trouble."

Blaze flapped his wings urgently and gave a sudden, loud hiccup.

"Fetch some water!" called Doctor Morel.

"I'm so sorry ..." groaned Sir Horatio, dashing to the tap.

HICCUP! This one was even stronger, and the magic blanket quivered and shook.

"Oh dear," gulped Doctor Clarice, trying to tuck it more tightly around the little bird.

HICCUP! Blaze hiccuped again, and this time it was so strong that the blanket shot across the room and tore in two!

Rosie and Kat dived behind a table and threw their arms around each other!

HIC-HIC-HIC-HICCUUUUUUUUUP! Blaze gave one last, enormous hiccup. Rosie held onto Kat, and they both squeezed their eyes tightly shut.

"Oh no!" wailed Sir Horatio. "Not again …"

Rosie opened her eyes and saw that something strange had happened. Doctor Hart, Doctor Morel, Doctor Clarice, and Sir Horatio had all turned into toddlers! The gnomes' beards were gone, Doctor Hart's white hair had turned brown, and Doctor Clarice was rolling around the floor in a tiny little white labcoat.

Blaze gave a sorry squawk.

"Is everyone okay?" Rosie asked nervously.

Doctor Morel made a grab for Doctor Clarice's glasses, and she wriggled away. In a moment, the two vets were tumbling over each other in fits of giggles.

Little Doctor Hart clapped her hands in delight, and sat on the floor with a thump.

"Thilly billies," lisped Sir Horatio, throwing himself down beside Doctor Hart and wagging his finger at the others.

Kat looked at Rosie, and Rosie looked at Kat. They were now the most grown-up people in the room.

Rosie took a deep breath. She knew she had to stay calm. "We need to stop Blaze from hiccuping," she said.

"Yes," nodded Kat. "And fast."

"What worked for your brothers in the end?" asked Rosie.

"They got a shock," said Kat. "There was a sudden, loud noise and ..."

"Boombadger!" cried Rosie. "I'll go and find it. You get the blanket back on Blaze."

"Funny badger," burbled little Doctor Clarice. She grabbed hold of Rosie's leg to hitch a ride. "Wheeee!"

Somehow, Rosie made it into the main surgery with Doctor Clarice swinging on her leg. She looked around. There were cahoots, chamedeons, and smittens everywhere ... Where was the boombadger? At last, she saw it snuffling in a pile of pillows.

Rosie took a deep breath, picked it up, and ran back to Blaze.

The poor little bird was giving off bigger and bigger puffs of steam.

"It looks like he's working up to another hiccup," warned Kat.

Rosie plonked the boombadger next to Blaze. He flapped his wings in alarm.

HIC-HIC-HIC ...

"Please, please, please, little boombadger," urged Kat. "Do your thing."

The boombadger knew what to do. There was a tremendously loud BOOOOOM and a stinking cloud filled the room. It smelled of eggs, dirty socks, and cheese.

"Yikes!" gasped Rosie and Kat.

Blaze coughed, gasped, swayed—then flopped onto his back, his legs in the air.

"Blaze! Are you all right?" asked Rosie.

Blaze got to his feet and shook out his feathers. Then he began to sing a soft sweet rising tune. It was one of the most enchanting things that Rosie had ever heard.

As the girls watched in amazement, Blaze lifted his wings, sending out a shower of shimmering sparks. The sparks grew into magical golden flames, their smoke winding and circling until Blaze was hidden.

"His magic is working again!" gasped Rosie, gripping Kat's hand with excitement.

When the smoke cleared, Blaze was nowhere to be seen. But in his basket there was a large, scarlet egg ... and the girls could hear tapping coming from inside it.

A crack appeared in the egg, growing and spreading across the surface. Then the shell broke open and out hopped a bright red baby phoenix.

"It's baby Blaze!" said Kat.

Blaze gave a cheep. He took a wobbly step, then another, then another. Every step was stronger than the last.

"He's already learning to walk," said Rosie.

Now Blaze flapped his wings. He fluttered up to Rosie's shoulder, and nuzzled into her neck, with a happy chirrup.

Tingaling-tingaling-tingaling!

"Tee-hee," giggled little Doctor Hart. "Noisy noticeboard."

"Oh my goodness," sighed Kat. "We need to look after the other animals too!"

The girls went into the other room. The writing on the noticeboard read: *Trim the smittens' claws.*

"All right," said Rosie. She gently lifted Blaze off her shoulder and put him on the floor. Then she bent down to grab a scampering smitten. "I'll catch them while you trim them."

Kat picked up the clippers and sat on a stool beside Rosie. The silly smitten held both paws behind its back!

"Let's play a game," said Kat to the smitten. "Do you know your left from your right?" The smitten nodded proudly. "Show me your left paw." The smitten held out its left paw. "Very good," said Kat, giving the nails a clip. "Now which one is your right?"

As soon as the smitten was clipped, Rosie carried it into the examination room. The babies squealed in excitement and crawled over to play with it.

"That should keep everyone busy for a while," said Rosie, then went back to find a new smitten. Soon, they had clipped every smitten's claws.

The toddlers in the examination room were having a great time tumbling around the floor with the smittens. It sounded like a lot of fun! Kat and Rosie wished they could join in ... but they had more work to do.

Tingaling-tingaling-tingaling!

Now the noticeboard read: *Blow the cahoots' noses.*

Grabbing paper handkerchiefs, the girls leaped after the sneezing cahoots.

Blaze was growing up fast, and his confidence was growing too. He was taking longer and longer flights and he seemed to enjoy fluttering among the cahoots.

Rosie soon realized that it was best to jump into the air a second after each cahoot, so she could blow its beak on the way back down. Bounce and blow, bounce and blow, until her legs started to ache.

Tingaling-tingaling-tingaling!

More words appeared on the noticeboard: *Tidy up the chamedeons' patterns.*

"Oh no," groaned Rosie. All she wanted to do was sit down and take a break. She picked up the broom and swept up the spots and stripes. Kat fetched a dustpan and took the tidy piles to the trash.

"Look at Blaze," Rosie said suddenly. The phoenix had fluttered over to the window.

He looked out of the window at the wide blue sky and the waving trees.

"Should we let him out?" asked Rosie.

"I don't know," said Kat. "He's grown so big, but that doesn't mean he's ready to go out into the world alone."

They looked at each other nervously, both thinking the same thing. This was a question for one of the vets ... But the vets were in no state to make important decisions!

Rosie and Kat peeped around the door of the examination room. What a mess! Chairs had been tipped over. Pillows and blankets were strewn around the floor. The tiny vets were lying happily on the floor in a pile of smittens. Sir Horatio had found a pen and was busily writing his name on the wall.

"Izzit snack time?" asked Doctor Morel hopefully.

Kat went to the kitchen to find some juice and cookies, while Rosie took the pen away from Sir Horatio. Blaze stopped looking out of the window and swooped across the room, landing on Rosie's shoulder.

"Aw! He still wants to play with his friends," said Kat, picking up a cuddly cahoot.

"I know how you feel, Blaze," Rosie said. stroking his feathery head. "I don't think I'm quite ready to grow up yet, either."

Chapter 9
Giving a Present

"**We** can't thank you enough, dearies," said Doctor Hart, straightening her flowery hat. All the adults were back to their normal selves again—much to Kat and Rosie's relief.

"Without your quick thinking, Blaze would still be hiccuping," said Doctor Clarice, giving the girls a hug.

"And Sir Horatio would still be drawing on the wall," added Rosie with a giggle.

Sir Horatio looked embarrassed. "I'm sorry for all the trouble I caused," he said into his beard. "When I was little and ... er ... when I was big, too."

Doctor Clarice smiled. "Well, I think you've learned a lesson."

"Yes, yes," said the old gnome. "I, Sir Horatio Hornswaggle, Knight of the Order of the Green Garter, solemnly swear to never, ever, feed one of my pepperpears to a phoenix again!"

"Oh my spoons and jars! I'm very glad to hear that," said Doctor Morel.

Rosie and Kat said their goodbyes, climbed the twisting stairs, and stepped out of the oak tree into the sunny wood.

Quibble waved to them from the top of his wooden ladder. He was peering into the tree, where the flutterpuffs' striped cocoons were swinging on their threads.

"Just in time, just in time," he creaked. "They're coming out!"

Each cocoon started to quiver as the flutterpuffs inside broke free from the threads.

"I wonder if we'll recognize them now they're grown up," murmured Rosie.

All at once, the cocoons began to burst open. First one flutterpuff flew out, then another and another ...

"They're so pretty," squealed Kat.

To Rosie's amazement, they looked almost the same as before—except now, their fluffy

bodies sparkled in the sunlight, glittering with gold and silver speckles.

"You weren't growing up at all," laughed Rosie. "You just felt like being glittery!"

Squeaking excitedly, the flutterpuffs flitted around the girls' heads. Quibble's moss-tache twitched with happiness.

"I wish I could sparkle like that," said Kat, twirling around and around like the little flutterpuffs.

"I'd rather be able to wrap myself up in slumberfluff and sleep," laughed Rosie. It really had been a tiring few days!

Rosie and Kat ran all the way home through Starfall Forest. The Toad Gate clanged shut behind them, and they were back in Rosie's garden. After saying goodbye to Kat, Rosie bounded into the kitchen. She smiled to see all the boxes of cheesecakes on the counter, ready for the fundraiser.

Dad was still rehearsing for the show, humming whenever he couldn't remember the words. He smiled sheepishly as Rosie

came in. "You know I said I didn't need your help to learn the lyrics?" he said. "Well, is that offer still open?"

"Of course," laughed Rosie. "But there's something important I have to do first." She raced up to her room. There was the bag, just as she had left it. Gently, she took out all of her toys and put Duffy the fluffy duck back on her pillow, where he belonged.

She spent the rest of the afternoon helping Dad rehearse. "I had no idea you were such a good teacher," he said. "You really are growing up fast."

"Not too fast, I hope," laughed Rosie. "I've had quite enough of that for one day!"

The next day at the school fundraiser, Dad remembered every word and got a huge round of applause from the audience. And Mama's cheesecakes went down a storm, too!

After the fundraiser was over, the children spilled out into the schoolyard to play while the adults cleared up the hall. Rosie took Kat's hand and pulled her to the side. "I've got something for you," she said.

She handed Kat a gift wrapped in rainbow-covered paper. She had tied a purple ribbon around it in a bow.

"You got me a gift?" gasped Kat, carefully tearing off the paper. Inside was a pretty, sequinned notebook, which sparkled as it caught the sunlight.

"Look inside," said Rosie.

On the first page, Rosie had drawn a picture of Blaze, Kat, and Rosie. Blaze was flying around their heads, his red tail feathers whirling behind him. The rest of the pages were blank.

"It's lovely!" said Kat.

"It's a friendship journal," said Rosie. "It's somewhere we can keep a record of all the amazing things that we do together. I'm not in a rush to grow up any more ... I want to treasure every day."

Kat grinned happily. "We make a great team, don't we?" she said. "I couldn't have done all those crazy jobs without you."

"Me too," agreed Rosie. "I wonder if the smittens' claws have stopped growing yet?"

"I hope so," laughed Kat. "I don't want to clip any more claws for a looooong time."

In the middle of the schoolyard, the other children were holding hands and forming a big circle.

"What are they playing?" Rosie asked.

"It's called Boombadger Tag," said Kat. She giggled. "It's really fun! Of course, none of them have ever met a *real* boombadger ... Do you want to play?"

"I do!" said Rosie.

"Everyone can play," called Luca.

Rosie laughed with happiness. Suddenly, making new friends didn't seem quite so scary. The girls raced over to join the game.

"I'll be the Boombadger!" called Kat, running into the middle of the circle. She closed her eyes and started to count, and the other children scattered, screaming excitedly.

"You have to run away before she catches you," said Luca with a grin. "Come on!"

Rosie ran with him, dodging away from her friend when she came chasing after her. At last, Kat managed to catch Luca and he went into the middle of the circle to start the game all over again.

Suddenly, Rosie grabbed Kat's hand. "Look," she said. "It's just like my drawing …"

Blaze the Phoenix

Busy with their game, the other children did not notice the beautiful phoenix flying overhead. But there, high above the schoolyard, Blaze was swooping and soaring like a brilliant streak of scarlet. Stretching far behind him, over the trees of Starfall Forest, was a glowing trail of magical flames. The girls waved to their friend, and he flew in a perfect loop-the-loop, just for them.

"See you soon, Blaze!" whispered Rosie and Kat. They couldn't wait for the next time they visited the magical forest and had more exciting adventures.